KU-575-628

Zoë
and the Witches' Spell

Jane Andrews

Piccadilly Press • London

Zoë, Pip and the fairies were getting ready for a flying
competition with the witches. Everyone was very excited.
"You must all do your best," said the Fairy Queen.
"We want to bring the trophy back for *our* school
this year."

DUDLEY SCHOOLS
LIBRARY SERVICE

Zoë
and the Witches' Spell

Schools Library and Information Services

S00000645074

First published in Great Britain in 2002
by Piccadilly Press Ltd.,
5 Castle Road, London NW1 8PR

Text and illustration copyright © Jane Andrews, 2002

All rights reserved. No part of this publication may be reproduced,
stored in a retrieval system, or transmitted, in any form
or by any means, electronic, mechanical, photocopying
or otherwise, without prior permission of the copyright owner.

The right of Jane Andrews to be recognised as Author
of this work has been asserted by her in accordance with
the Copyright, Designs and Patents Act 1988.

Designed by Louise Millar
Printed and bound in Belgium by Proost

ISBN: 1 85340 731 3 (hardback)
1 85340 726 7 (paperback)

1 3 5 7 9 10 8 6 4 2

A catalogue record of this book
is available from the British Library

BUDLEY
L   46150
645074   SCH
JYAND

Jane Andrews has two sons and lives in
High Wycombe in Buckinghamshire.
Since graduating from art college she has
undertaken a variety of graphic work, including
illustrations for magazines.
Piccadilly Press also publish the other books in this series,
Zoë at Fairy School, **Zoë the Tooth Fairy**
and **Zoë and the Fairy Crown**:

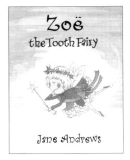

ISBN: 1 85340 640 6 (p/b)   ISBN: 1 85340 651 1 (p/b)   ISBN: 1 85340 644 9 (p/b)

The fairies flew off together. "I can't wait to see the forest and all the spring flowers," Zoë told Pip. "It's so beautiful at this time of year."

But as they approached the forest a
lightning bolt nearly struck the Fairy Queen!
Something was terribly wrong.

Inside the forest icicles hung from the branches
and snow was falling. The witches, however,
were laughing and flying about on their broomsticks.
"What is the meaning of this?" the Fairy Queen said.
"My fairies can't fly in this weather – their wings will
freeze! Why isn't the Head Witch here?"

The Head Witch finally arrived – late and very cross.
"If you girls did this to win the flying trophy you are
mistaken," she said. "Undo this spell on the forest right away!"

"But we didn't do anything!" the witches chorused.

"I'll try to put it right!" said one witch. "Kazzam!"
Suddenly the forest was full of bats – but it was still winter.

"Cadabra!" said another witch. Everyone suddenly had
long noses. Very cold, red, long noses!

Then all the little witches tried together. "Hocus pocus!"
. . . but a huge dragon appeared!
And it was as cold and miserable as ever.

So the Fairy Queen said, "Perhaps the fairies could try their magic."

"Wham!" tried the first fairy, and the air was filled with small teddy bears.

"Whoosh!" cried two other fairies, but the shooting stars and fireworks couldn't melt the icicles.

"Whizz!" All the fairies tried their hardest, but all that happened was that one tree sprouted lots of bananas!

"This is getting us nowhere," said the Fairy Queen. "The Head Witch and I will both try." But no matter what spell they tried, nothing worked!

Just then, Zoë saw puffs of purple smoke rising from behind some bushes.
"Quick, Pip! Follow me," she whispered.

Pip and Zoë found two little witches.
They were looking at a huge spell book and laughing.
"Oh Tabitha!" sniggered the tall, thin one, "they'll never unmake our spell! The forest will be in winter for ever!"
And the two little witches laughed some more.

"We must *do* something, Pip!" whispered Zoë.
"Quick, before they see us and cast a spell on us!
Let's turn them into toads! Then we can take them back
to the Fairy Queen."
"I'm not certain I can remember the spell," said Pip.
The two fairies whispered together, crossed their fingers
and raised their wands . . .

BANG! PLOP! The two little witches were turned into toads!

Zoë scooped them up and put them on the back of a broomstick. "Stay there!" she commanded. Pip balanced the big book of spells on the other broomstick, and they flew quickly back to join the others.

"It's Mo and Tabitha!" said the Head Witch. "I recognise their hats! And *this* is my great-grandmother's precious spell book! They must have taken it from my office and used it to cast a winter spell on the forest. They've broken every rule in the school. They'll have to remain toads for two whole weeks!"

The Head Witch flicked through the book,
muttering. Then, standing tall and holding
her arms out, she chanted loudly,
"Bang, whoosh,
kezazz, kerzing!"

Instantly the forest was transformed, filled
with springtime flowers and birds!

The fairies and the witches began their flying competition.

They did loops . . .

double loops . . .

and flying relays . . .

and with the witches' team two short, the fairies won easily!

Finish

"Congratulations to the fairies," said the Head Witch.
"And especially to Zoë and Pip. Without you,
the spell would never have been broken!"

And she handed them the biggest trophy they
had ever seen, to take back to the Fairy School!